W9-AVL-440

MIKE'S LONELY SUMMER

MIKE'S LONELY SUMMER

A Child's Guide: Divorce

By Carolyn Nystrom
Illustrated by Ann Baum

A LION BOOK

Published by
Lion Publishing
850 North Grove Avenue, Elgin, Illinois 60120, USA
ISBN 0 7459 2925 7

First edition 1985
This paperback edition 1994

10 9 8 7 6 5 4 3 2 1

Library of Congress CIP Data applied for

Printed and bound in Singapore

This is Mike. Mike is ten years old. Mike's Mom sells TV ads on Tuesdays and Fridays. She also makes the best spaghetti sauce in the world.

Mike's Dad teaches high school history during the week. But on Saturdays he coaches Mike's soccer team. On Sundays Mike's whole family goes to church.

Mike has a little brother named Jason. Jason is mostly good at making noise. He thinks he's a human fire truck.

Mike lives in a big brown house in the suburbs. He has grass and trees and a tire swing for sailing high and a sandpit for digging deep and sidewalks for skating fast and a cat named Abbey for petting and an old dog named Alex for curling up next to the fire.

But one spring a scary thing happened to Mike's family. Mike's Mom and Dad got a divorce.

Mike came home from school one day, threw his books on the kitchen table, and headed for his room to change for soccer practice. But his Dad called to him from the living room. Mike thought it was strange that Dad was home early. Then he saw that the rest of the family sat waiting for him. Mom and Dad both looked so serious that Mike's stomach did a flip-flop. Dad sat Mike next to him and Mom took Jason on her lap.

"Boys, we have something important to tell you," Dad began. Then he swallowed hard and looked at Mom. But Mom only looked down at her hands in her lap, so Dad went on. "Your Mom and I have been fighting a lot for a long time. You've probably heard us shouting at each other. We seem to always make each other angry."

Mike remembered the time Mom had thrown a cup of hot coffee at Dad and the time Dad had been so mad he shook the house when he slammed the back door. Then he screeched the car down the driveway.

Mom interrupted. "We love you, Mike, and we love you, Jason. You are our sons. But Dad and I don't love each other anymore. And we get so angry when we're together that we've decided we should live apart. Your Father will move to an apartment tomorrow. We are getting a divorce."

Then Mom and Dad stopped and looked at Mike as if they expected him to say something. Mike wished they had stopped a lot sooner—before they said that word *divorce*. A hundred questions came to his mind, but he couldn't think how to ask even one.

WHAT is a divorce?
Did I cause the divorce?
Can I fix the problem?
Who will take care of me?
Will I have to move?
Who will have my birthday party?
Is my Grandma still my Grandma if my Dad is gone?
Why is God letting Mom and Dad divorce?
Will Mom and Dad stop loving me, too?
Can I still love both my Mom and Dad if they don't love each other?
Will I have to take my Dad's place?
If I pray, will God bring Mom and Dad back together?
Who will make me be good?
Can I call my Dad if I need him?
Will I always feel this bad?

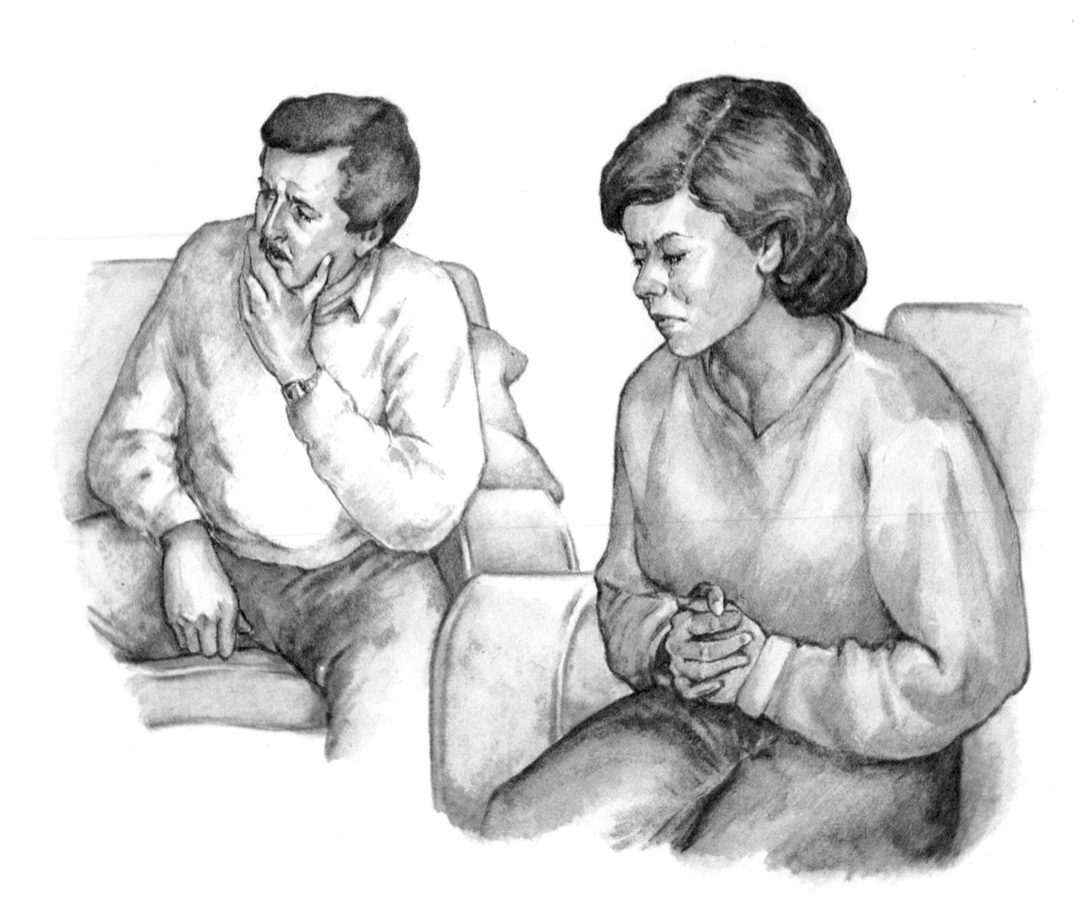

But pounding into Mike's head louder than any other question was "Why? Why? Why?" Then as he looked from Mom to Dad and back to each parent again, Mike wondered, "Why are Mom and Dad crying?"

DIVORCE is sad for everybody. It is sad for Mom and Dad. It is sad for Jason and Mike. It will be sad for Grandma and Grandpa. It will even be sad for friends.

Years ago, long before Mike was born, his Mom and Dad loved each other so much that they wanted to take care of each other forever. So they were married. God wants marriage to last all of our lives.

But after a while, Mike's Mom began to do what she wanted more than she took care of Dad. And Mike's Dad began to do what he wanted more than he took care of Mom. And soon they didn't love each other so much. Then it was even easier to be selfish. Finally, they didn't love each other at all.

But they hadn't expected their marriage to end that way. They are sad because now they can never do all the happy things they planned together. They are sad because of the lost love. And they are sad for their children: Mike and Jason will not have two parents together.

The next day, Mike's Dad drove into the driveway with a helper and a small truck. He loaded up the TV and the stereo. He took two lamps, lots of books and tapes, and all the clothes in his closet. He even went downstairs and took his tools from the workshop. Last, he got the dog leash and began to fasten it to Alex's collar.

Mike didn't say much, though he felt like Dad was taking his whole house apart. But when he saw Alex pad eagerly over to Dad for a "walk," Mike had to speak up. "Dad, please leave Alex with us. I love him."

Dad ruffled Mike's hair the way he always did when he was thinking. "Alright, Mike," he said. "I'll be lonely without Alex, but I guess you'll be lonely too."

Then Dad kissed Mike and Jason good-by. "You can come to visit me on Saturday," he said. But he didn't say anything at all to Mom. He just turned around and left. This time he closed the door softly.

That night, Dad's empty chair at the end of the table seemed bigger than all the rest. Mike didn't feel like eating supper. And the house looked so empty and strange that he didn't feel like playing either. Finally, he went to his room and closed the door. Abbey went with him. Mike liked the familiar smell of his own clothes and books and stuffed animals. He liked Abbey's soft purr as he stroked her tummy. Here, at least, home still felt like home.

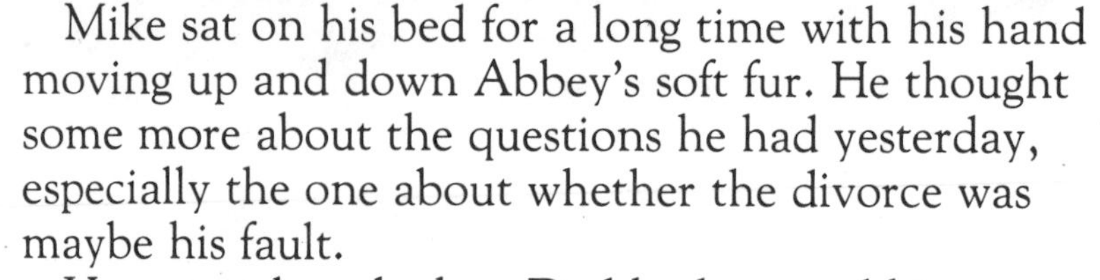

Mike sat on his bed for a long time with his hand moving up and down Abbey's soft fur. He thought some more about the questions he had yesterday, especially the one about whether the divorce was maybe his fault.

He remembered when Dad had wanted him to play soccer, but Mom thought piano was more important. They'd fought a long time about that. Maybe he should have just volunteered to do both.

Then there were the big arguments about his jobs. Mike was supposed to walk Alex right after school. But sometimes he forgot. Then if the dog made a mess, Dad got really mad. But he didn't yell at Mike. He yelled at Mom.

The more Mike thought those thoughts, the better the hard spot in his stomach felt. "If I caused the divorce," he thought, "then if I'm super, fantastic, extra-special good, then maybe, maybe, maybe, Mom and Dad will get back together."

MIKE'S idea won't work, because the divorce is not his fault. Kids don't cause divorce, and they can't fix it either. Parents divorce because of grown-up problems. So, no matter how much Mike tries, he can't get his family back together. As hard as it may seem, Mike will just have to get used to his Mom and Dad living in separate places.

That Saturday Mike and Jason visited Dad in his new apartment. It smelled like fresh paint and burnt toast. It seemed strange to see Dad's things from home in this new place.

Mike helped Dad hang pictures. Dad even let him help decide where they looked best. Dad made hamburgers and macaroni with cheese for lunch—Mike's favorite. Then they all played Monopoly. It was fun, except Jason kept getting mixed up.

By the time Dad dropped them off at the end of their driveway, Mike figured that maybe this divorce stuff wasn't so bad after all. It had been months since Dad had taken a whole day just for the boys. Besides, the apartment complex where Dad lived had an indoor swimming pool.

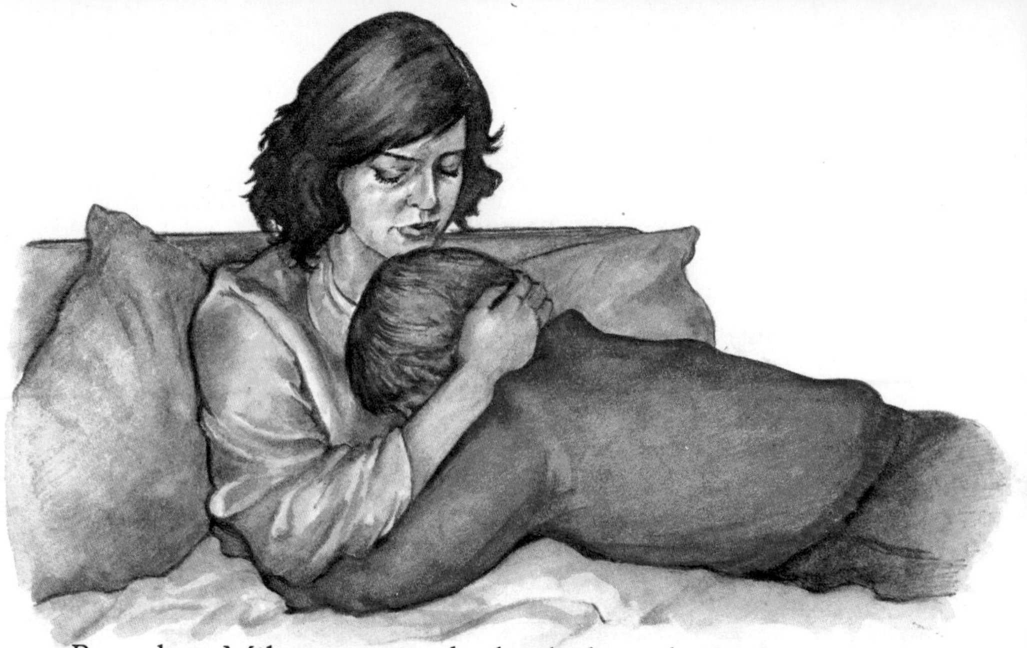

But when Mike came in the back door, he knew that something was wrong. The house was dark and quiet. Too quiet.

"Mom?" he said softly.

Then suddenly Mike felt scared. "Mom," he screamed and ran into her bedroom.

Mom was there alright. She sat up in bed looking a little pale.

"Mom, Mom," Mike cried, and hugged her. "I was so scared. I thought you were gone."

"No Mike, I love you and I won't leave you," Mom said. "I just wasn't feeling well today, so I took a nap. I'm sure I'll feel fine tomorrow. In fact, I'm feeling better already." Mike could see his knees begin to stop shaking, but he still felt scared.

"Mom," he asked, "what if something *did* happen to you? Who would take care of Jason and me?"

WHEN parents divorce, they can decide several different ways to take care of their children. Mike and Jason will live mostly with their mother, but will visit their father once a week. Other children may live with their father and visit their mother.

But children divide their time between parents in other ways too. Some children live the first part of the week with one parent and the second part with the other. Or they may live part of a year with one parent and the rest of the year with the other. Some children even stay in the same house all the time, but their Mom and Dad take turns staying with them.

Parents who divorce still want to take care of their children. But since Mom and Dad don't want to live together anymore, they have to take turns with the children.

Young children never have to take care of themselves. If Mom were not there, they would probably live with their Dad. But if they couldn't do that, their parents might arrange for an aunt or uncle or grandma, or even a good friend to take care of them.

Children get scared sometimes, though, if they are living with only one parent. They worry, "What if Mom were gone? Who would take care of me?" They won't feel so scared if they ask their parents for an answer.

That Sunday, Mike and Jason and Mom went to church just like always. They sat in the same seats they always did. But Dad's seat next to Mike was empty. Dad went to a different church.

People seemed extra friendly that day. Several people hugged Mom and said they were praying for the family. Mike's Sunday school teacher invited him to supper at his house later in the week. But Mike still felt like church wasn't church without Dad.

When it was time to pray, Mike thought an angry prayer to God, "God, you say you're in charge of everything, and you say you love me. Then why are you letting my Mom and Dad divorce? Don't you know I need them both?"

Just then Mike had another good idea. "Maybe I'll pray for God to make Mom and Dad live together again. God can do anything, can't he?"

MIKE is right about God. God can do anything. And it's alright to pray an angry prayer to God. God knows how we feel and he wants us to talk to him. So it would be silly to pretend to God that we feel happy if we're really mad and scared inside. We can say, ''God, I feel mad and scared, and here's why.'' Then tell him why.

But God probably will not make Mike's Mom and Dad live together. God lets people make many choices, even if those choices make God sad, or if the choices hurt other people. God often lets them do what they want anyway.

Maybe instead of asking God to make Mom and Dad live together again, Mike should pray for both his Mom and his Dad. It is a hard time for them too.

Tuesday after school Mike pedaled his bike fast down the last block of his paper route. The spring wind brushed cool through his hair. Lilacs and crab apples turned every yard into a perfumed fairyland.

Suddenly Mike felt a familiar ping behind his pedal and his feet flew effortlessly in a circle. His bike chain had popped. Mike took a deep breath, tried to drag a toe and took aim for a nearby bush that he hoped wasn't loaded with prickers.

A few seconds later he picked himself up, pulled his bike out of the bush, and brushed off a few broken branches. A huge scrape covered his right arm from elbow to wrist where he'd hit the sidewalk, and he felt a bruise on his left cheek. Otherwise, he didn't seem too hurt.

Mike walked his bike the rest of the way home, using his good arm to deliver the last five papers.

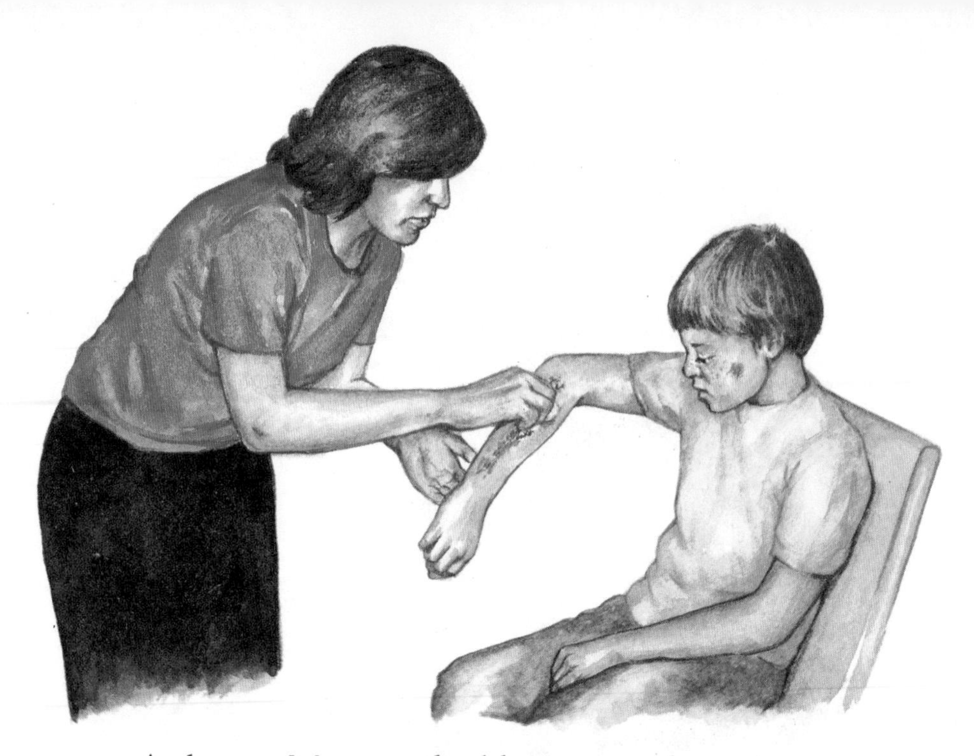

At home, Mom washed his arm with cool water, put ointment on it and checked to see if all of his body moved alright. She gave him an ice pack for his bruised cheek.

"When a guy gets himself banged up," Mike said, "what would he do without a mom?" And he hugged Mom as well as he could with his sticky arm.

But quick as a flash, his mind shifted to his Dad. "What about my bike?" he thought, as he remembered all the times he and Dad had worked together on his five-speed. "Dad always fixes the chain, and I don't know how. Neither does Mom."

Mike felt mixed up. "Can I still love both my parents, even if they don't like each other?"

MIKE can love both his parents. Mike's Dad is still his dad even if he isn't his Mom's husband. And Mike's Mom is still his mom, even if she isn't his Dad's wife. Mike has his Dad's brown hair, but he has his mother's blue eyes. He likes country music just like his Dad, but he also likes walking in the woods just like his Mom. Mike is like both his parents.

Even though Mike doesn't live with his Dad, he can call him whenever he wants. Mike can ask Dad to write his apartment and his school phone on two pieces of paper—one for him and one for Jason. (But the boys should not call him at work unless there is a serious problem that can't wait.) If Mike calls his Dad this week about his bike accident, his father will probably help him fix the chain when he visits on Saturday.

Children need both a mom and a dad, even if they can have only one at a time. So it is good for them to love both parents, even if the parents don't love each other.

By the time Dad had been gone a month, home began to feel a little more normal. Mom bought furniture from garage sales to fill the living room again. And she started working extra days at the TV station. On those days, Mike took a house key to school. When he got home, he stopped at the neighbors to pick up Jason. Then he unlocked the door and made a snack for both of them. Mom would call about then. It seemed she always told Mike, "Do your homework before TV." But Jason didn't have homework, so he got to play.

Mom was usually tired when she got home. Then she would ask Mike to set the table and take out the garbage, and maybe even help with supper. Since Mike didn't get homework on Fridays, Mom told him to mow the grass then.

Mike felt grown-up doing all those jobs that Dad used to do, but he also felt angry. Mowing the grass was kind of fun. But making a snack for his little brother and taking out garbage? Yuk! He'd rather play with his friends.

One day, after he'd done all those extra jobs, Mike didn't sit at his own place at the table. Instead, he sat in Dad's empty chair. "If I'm doing Dad's work," he grumbled to himself, "I might as well sit in his chair too."

But Mom looked straight at him and thundered, "Back to your own seat, Buster!"

Then she took Dad's chair away from the table and put it in the living room.

EVERYONE has extra work after a divorce. That's because there are two houses to take care of instead of one. Perhaps Dad did not cook or do laundry before. Now he has to do both. Mom has to work extra days. And she has to get the car fixed. Even children must do extra work too.

But Mike cannot take his Dad's place. He is still a boy and should let his parents take care of him. He should not pretend to be grown-up now. Growing up to be a man will come later.

But Mike should help his Mom and Dad in ways that a boy can help. He can keep Jason happy, mow the grass, clean his room, fold laundry, do his homework on time, and lots of other things that make his parents' work easier. Besides that, he can give them both a big hug, because they need extra loving now.

One Friday, Mike didn't feel like mowing grass. He didn't feel like picking up Jason either. It was nearly summer, and hot. What Mike felt most like doing was riding his bike with his friends to the corner store for a frosty drink. Mike didn't ask Mom—she wasn't home to ask. But Mike knew she'd say *no* because it would cost extra money to leave Jason at the neighbor's.

Mike left a note on the kitchen table and bicycled off. "Bicycling is lots more fun than walking behind a lawn mower," thought Mike. "For one thing, you don't get grass stuck to your sweaty legs."

But when Mike got home at supper time, Mom was furious. “What makes you think you can just take off without asking?” she yelled.

“What was I to think when I called and no one answered?” By then she was stamping her foot.

“Do you know, young man, that I had to leave work early *and* pay extra money for the baby sitter?”

Now Mom’s face was as red as any time that she’d yelled at Dad. “That, sir, is coming out of your allowance!”

Then she locked up his bike for a week.

That night Mike didn't feel like watching TV with Jason and Mom. Instead, he stayed in his room and tried to read. But a worrisome thought kept coming back to his mind. If Mom got mad at Dad and stopped loving him, would she also stop loving her son? Then what if Dad stopped loving him too?

MIKE'S Mom and Dad will not stop loving him. There are many different kinds of love. Mom love and Dad love is different from husband and wife love. Most parents love their children forever.

Mike's Mom was angry with him. But it was not the same kind of anger as she had for Mike's Dad. She was angry because Mike had done wrong. And her anger will teach Mike to do right next time. After all, he can't ride to the corner store without permission as long as his bike is locked. And he'll likely think twice before he skips his Friday work again. Even though Mike feels unhappy right now, his Mom is helping him to do good.

God will help Mike do what is right too. All Mike needs to do is ask.

Next day, Saturday, Mike and Jason went to Dad's for their regular visit. Grandma was there too. In the morning, Grandma let them help her bake cookies, cut them in funny shapes, then decorate them with squirty frosting and sprinkles. Mike liked his soldier cookie with a fancy uniform best. But Jason liked his cookie shaped like a truck.

In the afternoon Dad took them to a movie. Dad sat between them with a big tub of popcorn on his lap and they all ate until they were stuffed.

Walking out of the movie, holding onto Dad's big hand, Mike said, "I wish I could have Saturday every day." Then he wondered, "Why is Dad so nice and Mom so mean?"

MIKE'S Dad only sees his boys one day a week. So he can do all of his work when the boys are not there. It is easier for him to keep Saturday free as a fun day. But Mike's Mom takes care of them six days a week. This means she has to do all of her work while they are with her. She also has to teach the boys to do their work. Sometimes she gets tired and crabby.

But, if Mike thinks hard, he will remember fun times with his Mom too. Like the time Jason spilled a whole bowl of spaghetti all over himself and Alex. Alex looked so puzzled about the spaghetti hanging over his eyes that Mom burst out laughing. Then she hustled Jason and Alex outside and turned the garden hose on them both. Even Mike got to jump in the water.

Perhaps when Mike is going to sleep each night, he can try to remember one happy thing he did with a parent that day—even if it's something small like a short talk about something they enjoy, or maybe a quick hug on the way out the door. Then he can thank God for that.

One day at school, Mike found a good reason to feel glad his Mom is his Mom, and his Dad is his Dad.

Nicole is new at school, so Mike stayed in from recess one day to help her catch up in long division. Later they talked about families.

Nicole lives alone with her Dad. A year ago, Nicole heard her parents fighting in the night. When she got up in the morning, her mother was gone. She sent Nicole one postcard with a picture of a sunny beach. Nicole wrote three letters to her Mom, but her Mother never answered. And she never comes to visit. So Nicole wonders if her Mom loves her.

Besides that, Nicole's Dad says mean things about her Mom like, "Your Mother, the slob," and, "Now don't grow up to be witchy, like your Mother."

Nicole feels sad a lot of the time. She remembers good things about her Mother, and she misses her. But she can't tell her Dad how she feels because he would get angry. When Nicole looks in the mirror she sees her own dark hair and deep brown eyes and she knows inside that she is much like her Mother. Nicole loves her Dad too, but she wishes he wouldn't say mean things about her Mom.

After listening to Nicole, Mike was glad he has a Mom and Dad who both love him—even if they don't live together. But he wondered about Nicole's family. Do some parents stop loving their children?

NICOLE'S Mother has a problem, but so does her Dad. And together they are making their divorce much harder for Nicole.

It's hard to know why Nicole's Mom does not visit or write. But Nicole is right to wonder if her Mother loves her. Maybe her Mom has good reasons, but perhaps not.

Sometimes a parent gets so used to being selfish, that he or she is selfish even with the children. Maybe Nicole's Mom doesn't want the work of taking care of a little girl, and just wants to be alone. Maybe she really doesn't love Nicole as much as she should.

But that doesn't mean other people won't love Nicole. It is her Mother who has the problem with love, not Nicole. Nicole might like to find a substitute mom, like an aunt or grandma, for special girl-woman times. Then she won't miss her own Mom so much.

But Nicole's Dad has a problem too. Even if he does not love Nicole's Mom anymore, he should notice that it hurts Nicole when he says bad things about her. Nicole's Mom will always be her Mom, even if she hardly ever sees her. Perhaps her Dad will listen to Nicole if she chooses a quiet time to explain how sad his criticism makes her feel.

Since both of Nicole's parents give her problems, it will help her to know that Mike is her friend. And Mike can remind her that God loves her too.

Spring ended and so did school. Mike and Jason spent more time with Dad because he was out of school too. Mike climbed trees and rode his bike and played baseball and sailed high in the tire swing. Sometimes he played "big truck" with Jason in the sand pit. Sometimes they fought, but other times they hugged.

It was not the same as other summers. Mom worked harder, and Dad looked sad. And one of them was always missing. Whenever Mike looked at Dad's empty chair, he wondered if the rock hard lonely spot in his stomach would ever go away.

One night, just before school started, Mike talked with his Dad about those lonely empty feelings. Jason was asleep, snoring softly because of a stuffy nose, but Mike laid in bed and stared at the ceiling. He tried to imagine pin prick stars over his head, but all that he saw was black above him. The only light in his room cracked in under the door.

Finally, he got up and padded through the apartment looking for Dad, but the rooms were all empty. Just as Mike started to feel a little frightened, he heard soft radio music coming from the tiny balcony off the living room. Mike slid the door open and stepped out. His Dad sat leaned back in a lawn chair while a voice on the radio sang something about a lonesome cowboy.

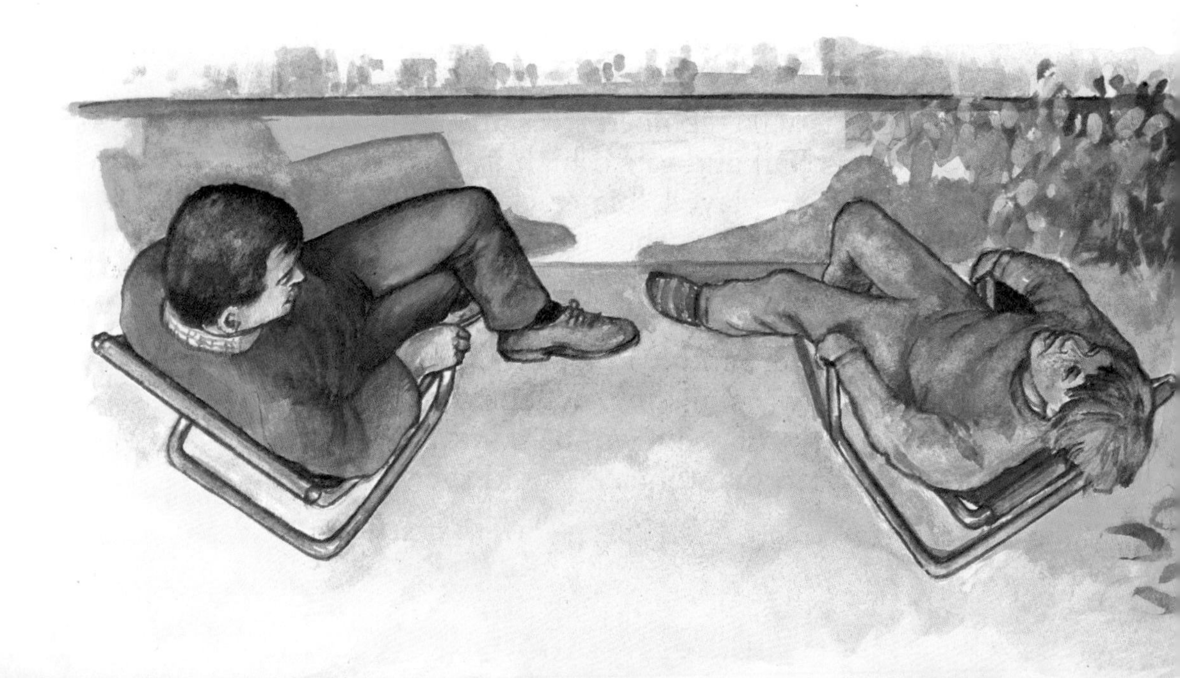

"Hi, son," Dad said and motioned Mike to the chair next to him. "Feeling lonesome?"

Mike nodded and sat down.

"Me too," Dad said.

Mike rested his neck against the back of his chair and looked up. Millions of stars dotted his whole range of vision—much better than the black ceiling of his room.

"It's hard to have only one parent at a time," Mike said softly. "I love you both."

"I know," Dad said. "All of us are more lonely now." Dad reached over and took Mike's hand. "But we can ask God to fill some of our empty spots."

Both Mike and his Dad were quiet for a while. They looked up at the stars and listened to traffic sounds below them. Mike let his mind pray a mixed-up lonely prayer.

Finally Mike's Dad spoke softly. "I was just thinking. In many ways God is like a parent to us. The Bible even uses parent names to talk about God."

"What does it say?" Mike asked. Maybe God really could help him feel less alone.

"In some places, the Bible says that God is a Father," Dad answered. "He even invites us to be in his family. But the Bible also says that God is like a mother. It says that God holds us and takes care of us just like a mother cuddles her tiny baby."

"I wish I could see God and touch him like I can see and touch you and Mom," Mike said.

"I know," Dad answered. "God just isn't like us in that way. But there are other ways that God isn't like us too. God doesn't change like we do. When God loves us, he loves us for ever and ever and ever. And God will never, ever leave us alone."

Mike and his Dad watched the stars together for a long time that night. Sometimes they talked, but mostly they just sat quietly in the dark. When Mike was almost asleep, he felt his Dad gather him up in his arms and carry him to bed.

DIVORCE is sad for everyone—and it doesn't go away. Even after Mike is grown up, he will always feel a little sad about the divorce. But parents are not perfect, and neither is Mike. Only God is perfect. Because God loves him, Mike can keep on loving his Mom. And his Dad. And Jason. And Mike can even love himself.